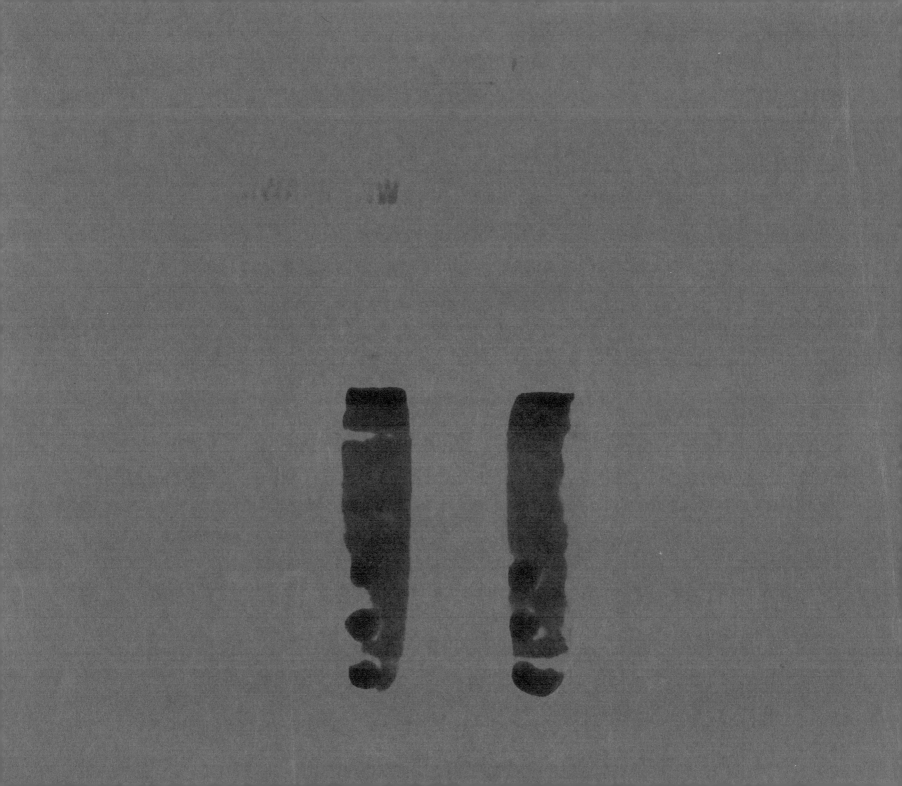

First there was Frances

For Fay, the only person I ever saw with a Shetland pony in her kitchen.

Library of Congress Cataloging-in-Publication Data: Graham, Bob. First there was Frances. Summary: Frances lives alone in plenty of space at the edge of the city, but is joined, one at a time, by so many other people and animals that they all move to the country. [1. Family life—Fiction] I. Title. II. Title: Frances. PZ7.G75166Fi   1986   [E]   85-17141   ISBN 0-02-737030-5

First there was Frances

Bob Graham

BRADBURY PRESS · NEW YORK

First there was Frances.

Frances lived alone. There was a long wooden fence near her house,

and over the fence was the city.   *Then* came . . .

Graham.

Graham worked at the airport. He caught a dog chasing planes.

The dog was shaggy and red, the color of rust.

They called him Teak.

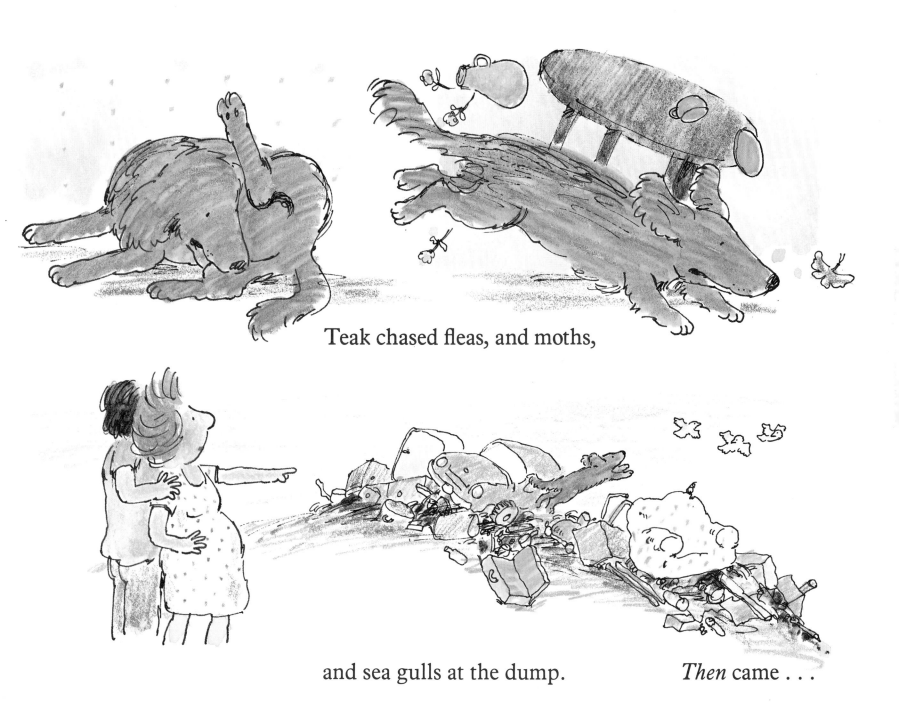

Teak chased fleas, and moths,

and sea gulls at the dump.   *Then* came . . .

Marisol, and then Fraser.

Marisol and Fraser liked to go riding with Frances and Graham,

and Teak.   *Then* came . . .

Grandma.

Grandma lived in her own van.

She grew vegetables and little red flowers.

She watered them every day.

But Teak trampled Grandma's vegetables.
Then came . . .

Katy the goat.

Katy lived in the laundry, and ate cake.

She also ate Grandma's flowers.

Then came . . .

the Guinea pigs, Errol and Berryl.

They ate lettuce and long grass.

Their cage was moved every day.
There were patches in the lawn.

Then came . . .

Triller the canary. Grandma bought him in a pet shop.

Triller would not sing. He looked miserable.

Grandma gave him dandelions.

He was moulting and his feathers went everywhere.
He looked like he was wearing someone else's clothes.

Then came . . .

Nugget the billy goat. He was fierce and smelly.

He nearly pinned Fraser to the gate.

Nobody liked Nugget except Katy.

Frances rescued Fraser just in time.

Then came . . .

Toyful the alley cat.

Toyful could not reach Triller the canary.

She leapt wildly at Katy the goat.

Katy lifted her high in the air,
but Toyful landed on her feet.
Then came . . .

the baby goats, Ruby, Earl and Curl.

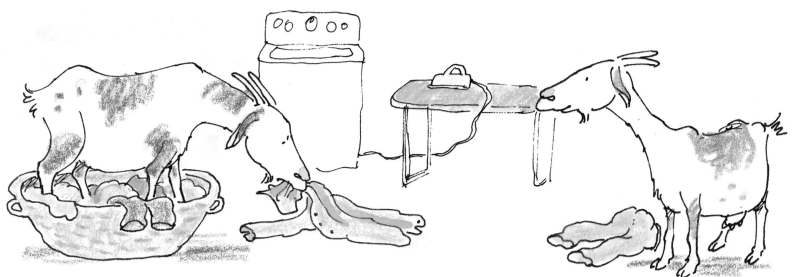

Nugget tried to move into the laundry with Katy.

He made Graham's shirts smelly.   *Then* came . . .

the Guinea pig babies.

One was called Smokey,
and the other, Hazel.

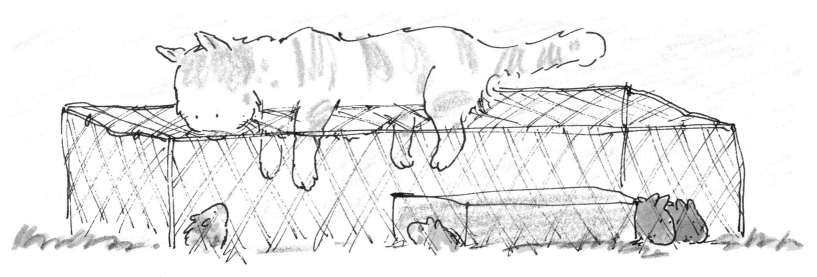

Toyful tried hard to catch them.   So *now* there were . . .

Frances and Graham, Teak, Marisol, Fraser, Grandma, Triller, Toyful,
Errol and Berryl, Smokey, Hazel, Katy, Nugget, Ruby, Earl and Curl.

That's not counting the black cat Puma,
who came to live in the cupboard,

and her kitten Barnaby.
Also the ferret Nosy with his little pink eyes.

They learned to live together in their back garden near the city.

Teak caught his fleas and moths, but never caught a sea gull. Triller grew his feathers and sang again. Smelly Nugget moved into the laundry with Katy.

Graham kept his shirts out of the laundry.

They watched Toyful the cat very carefully near the Guinea pigs.
Grandma built a fence around her vegetables . . . and *then* came the horses.

That's when they moved
to the country.